Feb2016

THIS BOOK BELONGS TO

D1235191

PUFFIN BOOKS

Published by the Penguin Group
Melbourne • London • New York • Toronto • Dublin
New Delhi • Auckland • Johannesburg • Beijing
Penguin Books Ltd, Registered Offices: 80 Strand, London WC2R 0RL, England
Published by Penguin Group (Australia), 2014
10 9 8 7 6 5 4 3 2 1

Printed and bound in Australia by McPherson's Printing Group, Maryborough, Victoria
National Library of Australia Cataloguing-in-Publication data available.
ISBN 978 0 14 330764 8

puffin.com.au
ouraustraliangirl.com.au

Charms on the front cover reproduced with kind permission from A&E Metal Merchants.
www.aemetals.com.au

OUR
AUSTRALIAN
GIRL

Daisy All Alone

It's 1930 and Daisy's worst nightmare has come true. She's alone on the streets, separated from her family. Things get worse after the police send her to live at the Melbourne Orphanage. At least she doesn't have to scavenge for food scraps anymore, but with no family and no freedom, Daisy is miserable. When she hears some shocking news she decides it's time to plot a daring escape...

Follow Daisy on her adventure in the second of four exciting stories about a hopeful girl in troubled times.

Puffin Books

For Jaime Mae

OUR
AUSTRALIAN
GIRL

Daisy
All Alone

Michelle Hamer

With illustrations by Lucia Masciullo

Puffin Books

Where this story takes place

Daisy's life in the country changed forever
when Dad lost his job because of the Great
Depression. She and her little sister,
Flora, were sent to live with their horrible
Aunt May in Melbourne while Dad looked for
work. He promised to write and send money,
but no letters ever arrived, and Aunt May
became more and more angry...

Thank goodness for Mabel and Elsie, the
twins from down the street, who taught Daisy
the tricks of city living. But when Aunt
May decided that she wanted to keep Flora
and bring her up as a proper lady, she and
Daisy came to blows. Now Daisy is out on the
street, alone, and night is falling fast...

1
Dudley Flats

'Now where am I supposed to go?' Daisy shouted. 'You wicked woman!' There was no response from behind the firmly shut door of her aunt and uncle's cottage.

Daisy stared up and down the laneway in shock, her heart thumping. How could Aunty May just throw me out? she wondered. It's not our fault that Dad hasn't sent her money to look after us. And why does she adore Flora so much when she obviously can't stand me?

Daisy looked down the empty lane, unsure of where to go. It was almost dark and there were strange noises coming from a clump of bushes nearby. I'll probably get slashed by a razor gang or murdered by a gangster like that Siddy Kelly, Daisy thought. Uncle Bertie had told her about gangsters who attacked people on the streets at night with cut-throat razors. She jumped as a man walked past.

'Nothing to worry about, missy,' the man said, 'I'm just out for me evening stroll.'

'Oh ... thank you,' Daisy stuttered. Too scared to stay in the dark lane alone, she ran to her friends Mabel and Elsie's house, and banged on the door. They always knew what to do.

'Whoever is it at this hour?' she heard the twins' mother call.

'I'll get it, Ma,' Mabel answered and a second later the door was flung open. 'Daisy!'

'Can I come in, Mabel?' Daisy asked, her teeth starting to chatter with cold and worry.

'Course.' Mabel stood back to let Daisy into a dimly lit room that stank of boiled cabbage.

Daisy had never been into the twins' house before, and by the looks of it, they were even poorer than she had imagined.

'Ooh!' Elsie appeared from the hallway. 'Come to sit in the parlour and take tea, have you, my dear?' But she stopped when she saw Daisy's face. 'You do look pale. What's the matter?' Elsie asked, moving to give Daisy a hug.

'I had a big fight with Aunty May and she threw me out, and, and . . .' Daisy couldn't talk any more. Her throat had grown tight and sore.

'That awful cow!' Mabel cried.

'And Flora?' Elsie asked. 'I'll throttle that old bag if she harms a hair on that girl's head.'

'Flora's fine,' Daisy said. 'Aunty May kicked me out so she could have Flora to herself. She wants to bring her up as her own daughter.' Daisy felt her voice crack with tears. 'I can't make Flora live on the streets with me. It's better that she stays with Aunty May until I find Dad.'

'But where will you go?' Mabel cried.

'Well, she'll stay with us, of course,' Elsie said, jumping up. 'I'll go and ask Ma right now.'

A glimmer of hope shone in Daisy's mind.

Elsie raced off and was soon whispering loudly to her mother in the kitchen.

'Where on earth would we put one more body, child?' Mrs Roberts said. 'I can't feed the lot of you as it is. I'm sorry, dear.'

Daisy hung her head and let her hair drop around her face to hide her burning cheeks.

'Sorry,' Mabel whispered.

'But Maaaaaa,' Elsie whined.

'That's enough of that carry on,' her mother hissed. 'Now look. My old friend, Mrs Owens, has a hut down in Dudley Flats, and it's only her there now. I'm sure she'd give your friend a place to shelter until she can make other plans.'

Daisy felt cold and prickly all over. Dudley Flats was little more than a garbage dump.

Elsie walked sadly into the room. 'Did you

hear that? Sorry, Daisy. I did my best. Mabel and me can walk to Dudley Flats with you. We'll have to hop a tram part of the way 'cos it's a fair old hike, right on the other side of the city and pretty dodgy at this time of night.'

Daisy just nodded, feeling as if all her words were turning to dust in her mouth.

An hour later, the trio stood, hand-in-hand, surveying the dismal, muddy fields of Dudley Flats, the scruffy shantytown where many of the city's homeless people lived. There were whole families packed into the shacks on the boggy marsh. Daisy's feet felt as heavy as lead.

'Come on,' Elsie said. 'I've been to Mrs Owens's before – it's down here.' She pointed at a messy group of huts only just visible in the moonlight.

'What's she like, Mrs Owens?'

'Oh, she's all right. Not the cheeriest bird in

the nest, but harmless enough,' said Mabel.

Soon they were standing by a small shanty, not much higher than Daisy's head. I can't believe someone actually lives in there, she thought. It looks like the cubby house Amelia's dad built. The memory of her best friend made her ache with sadness. Amelia had kept her word and written to Daisy every week since she and Flora had left the farm twelve weeks ago. What a perfect life I had back then, Daisy thought sadly. My best friend right next door, Dad and Flora there with me, and Jimmy, my beautiful horse, in his paddock.

But that was before Daisy's dad had lost his job and everything changed. Daisy sighed. And now I'm here all alone, she thought.

'Daisy, wake up!' Mabel said and tugged at her arm. 'You're in a complete daze.'

'Sorry,' Daisy answered.

Mabel rubbed her arm. 'We'll help find your dad, and we'll tell Flora what's happened, too.'

'Thanks,' Daisy said. 'But please don't tell Flora I'm here – she'll be ever so worried. Just tell her I'm staying with a friend of yours, will you? And that I'll be back soon, and to be good.'

'Will do,' Mabel said, and gave Daisy a hug. 'We'll come and see you soon, and it can't be too long before a letter comes from your dad. We'll ask Flora to let us know if it arrives. Maybe he's struck it rich on the goldfields and soon you'll be living like some fancy toff in a grand mansion.'

Daisy squeezed Mabel's hand. She was glad to have made such good friends in the city.

Elsie banged on the tin door of the shanty.

'Yeah, what?' a voice called from inside.

'Err ... Mrs Owens, it's Mabel and Elsie Roberts. Our ma said you might have room in there for our friend who has nowhere to stay.'

Mrs Owens pulled the piece of tin aside and stood bent over in the low doorway. Her face looked creased and tanned like an old leather shoe. Daisy noticed a layer of grime was etched into the lines on her face and under her nails.

'So you need somewhere to stay, do ya?' Mrs Owens asked, looking at Daisy.

'Ye-es,' Daisy answered. 'Yes please.'

'Well, me daughter's gone and got herself hitched to some bloke from Sydney, so I could do with the company. But I won't be feeding ya, and I've got no money, so you can forget any ideas of stealing from me.'

'She's okay,' Mabel said. 'Our ma said to tell you she would vouch for her.'

'Well, all right then,' Mrs Owen said. 'Welcome to my grand Dudley Mansion.'

Daisy gave the twins one more hug, and took the piece of bread and the flour sack they'd given her. She tried hard to smile. 'Bye girls, please visit me soon. I won't be able to find my way back to Gertrude Street, and I want to come up with a plan to find Dad right away.'

'No worries,' Mabel said.

'We've got double shifts the next two days, but we'll come after that,' Elsie added.

With a wave, the twins disappeared into the darkness and Daisy was left with Mrs Owens.

Daisy looked her up and down, and sighed. Well, at least she doesn't seem like the type to slit my throat while I sleep, she thought. I guess I'll have to make the best of things for now.

She dipped her head to fit under the low door. Inside the hut was a small table made from half an old door balanced on a pile of bricks. Upturned fruit crates acted as chairs. A small candle threw long shadows on the wall. There was a pile of newspaper and a bundle of old rags on the floor where Mrs Owens slept.

'You can sleep in that corner,' the woman said, pointing to a dark spot behind the table.

Daisy was too tired to do anything but pull some sheets of newspapers on top of the dirt and throw the flour sack over herself. Within minutes, she was asleep in the dark, cold hut.

2
Raided!

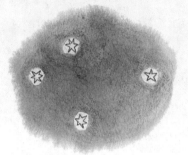

DAISY clung tighter to Jimmy's mane. Her hair billowed wildly behind her as they galloped through the paddock. If only it weren't so cold, Daisy thought, leaning closer to Jimmy for warmth. It felt like ice water was rushing through her veins instead of blood.

'I'm freezing,' Daisy muttered to herself over the steady pounding of Jimmy's hooves.

'Oi, get off me girl, and stop your jibbering. A woman can't sleep with that going on.'

Daisy sat up fast, her heart thumping. Where was she? Where was Jimmy? She blinked into the darkness as a horrible realisation slowly wrapped around her. She was in Dudley Flats, alone. A sob sprang from her lips.

'I warn you, urchin, one more sound and I'll box your ears,' Mrs Owens threatened.

'Sorry,' Daisy whispered, her voice thick with sadness as she shuffled away from the woman. She was still shivering with cold and realised she'd been trying to huddle up to Mrs Owens in her sleep.

'Shut up or get out,' Mrs Owens muttered.

As Daisy's eyes adjusted to the darkness, she could make out the shape of the table and fruit boxes. It was her fourth night in the shantytown, and there'd been no sign of Mabel or Elsie since they'd dropped her off.

Rain drummed on the flimsy wooden boards above her and Daisy realised that was the sound she'd heard in her dream. Patches of weak dawn light began to appear through the cracks in the roof where fat raindrops leaked in.

The last of the stars were fading. Daisy was too cold to sleep anymore. She stood up and tried to shake out the pins and needles that filled her legs like fizzy lemonade. She crouched low and groped for the makeshift door. Shifting the tin quietly, she crept out into the silent dawn.

The rain was easing to a miserable drizzle that made the view outside even bleaker than usual. *I thought it was bad at Aunty May's*, Daisy thought, *but this is much, much worse.*

She pictured Flora, asleep on Aunty May's couch, with food in her belly and a blanket to keep her warm. *At least she'll be looked after until I can come up with a plan to rescue her*, Daisy thought. She gritted her teeth. She'd get her family back no matter what. But where should she start? All she knew was that Dad was somewhere in the bush. She could try to kidnap Flora from Aunty May's, but then where would they go? Sometimes she dreamed of trying to get to Amelia's house, but how would she pay the train fare back to Healesville? And they couldn't live in Amelia's barn forever.

The angry growling of Daisy's stomach interrupted her thoughts. She couldn't save anyone if she starved to death. They'd probably just throw my body on the tip with all the other stuff no one wants. Tears rolled down her cold face and she shook herself. Moping wasn't going to help her now.

Daisy thought about the shelf of adventure stories at the farm that had been her mother's when she was a girl. She couldn't remember much about Mum, but when she closed her eyes and concentrated, she could still hear her reading aloud as they snuggled by the hearth in the wintertime. The girls in those stories always had lots of perils to overcome. Like them, Daisy had to be brave and strong.

'Right,' she said to herself, 'I am a heroine in an adventure, and I need to save my sister from an evil queen.' Her stomach rumbled again.

'But first I need breakfast.' She began picking her way through the boggy ground. By now she was used to the ugly collection of huts built out of scraps scavenged from the nearby tip. Most looked like they were about to collapse.

A foul smelled tickled at her nostrils and she knew she was getting close to the tip, the main source of food and supplies for the desperate Dudley Flats community.

On the first morning after Mabel and Elsie had brought her here, Daisy had watched in horror as whole families clambered over the rubbish, clawing for the smallest scraps.

Daisy had sat away from the rotting pile, refusing to believe she'd ever be desperate enough to pick through it for food. Stealing from bins at the Victoria Market with the twins was one thing, but sifting through a mound of putrid rubbish was another altogether.

But by the second day Daisy was too hungry and tired to care where she got her food from, and now she was used to scrounging for anything to fill the aching emptiness inside.

She put her hand over her nose as she got to the edge of the huge pile of garbage, and kicked away some rusty cans and empty bottles. The sky was brightening, but the world was still sleeping, except for one or two skinny stray dogs that sniffed hopefully at the rubbish.

Please just let me find one piece of food, something that's not rotten or filled with maggots, Daisy thought.

The smell was terrible, and blowflies droned around her, but she kept fishing through the old newspapers and rotting vegetables.

'Aha!' she exclaimed, pulling out a shrivelled potato. 'You'll make a perfect breakfast.' Daisy rubbed the dirt off and put it in her pocket.

The memory of her father's strong hands digging potatoes on the farm flooded her mind. She could almost smell fresh earth, feel the sun on her back and see her father's smile clearly. Oh Dad, she thought, what's happened?

She took a deep breath and leaned down to push back a piece of tin with both hands, grunting with the effort. The rain had started falling harder again, slicking her hair to her face in thick, wet strands. 'Come on,' Daisy panted, pushing at the tin again. She gave it one final shove, and the tin suddenly slid to one side, sending Daisy face forward into the garbage.

She felt something slimy and wet on her face, and put her hand in a sticky patch as she tried to push herself up.

'Oooh, *disgusting*,' she groaned.

She finally stood and held her face up to the sky to wash off the slime. A stab of fear went through her. The potato! Her hand flew to her pocket, but it was still there. That will have to do. I've had enough scavenging for one day.

But just as she was turning to leave, she noticed the glint of something shiny. Daisy reached through layers of rubbish to grasp hold of the shiny object and pull it out.

She gasped. It was a small, dented biscuit tin with a bright picture of a parrot on the front. She wiped the dirt from the tin and forced open the lid. Excitement shot through her like a firework. There were a few broken biscuits left in the tin.

Oh my *goodness*, Daisy thought as her sadness slid away. She stuffed two biscuits into her mouth, crumbs spraying. They were stale and hard, but to Daisy they tasted like birthday cake, ice cream and sweets all rolled into one.

Today is going to be a good day, I can feel it! she thought. I'll bet the twins will finally come to see me and we'll come up with the perfect plan for finding Dad. She jumped down from the rubbish heap and washed the potato in a puddle, then rinsed the lid of the tin as well.

Mrs Owens was still asleep when Daisy returned. She crept to her corner and carefully filled the tin with Amelia's letters, the photo of Jimmy and the clipping from his mane that Amelia had given her. She closed the lid and hugged it to her.

A scream of sirens suddenly split the dawn and Mrs Owens immediately jumped up and groped for the door. 'It's the coppers, girl. Run, run!' she cried.

Daisy peered outside to see a line of police cars parked on the edge of the muddy field, their sirens shrill in the early morning air. The huts around them erupted as people poured out clutching ragged possessions. 'What is it? What's happening?' Daisy asked.

'It's a bloomin' raid,' Mrs Owens answered, grabbing some rags and one of the fruit crates. 'The coppers don't like us living here so they come and flatten the huts every coupla months.'

She pushed past Daisy. 'Stay clear for a day or two, then everyone will be back building their mansions again,' she said, hobbling out into the rain.

Daisy was too shocked to move. Where could she go? Policemen in metal helmets began streaming from the cars and running towards the huts, yelling loudly at the inhabitants to clear out. As they reached the shanties, the police attacked the rickety homes with their batons, quickly knocking them to the ground.

Why was this happening? No one here was doing anything wrong. Daisy was still rooted to the spot when two policemen barreled up.

'What do we have here?' one of them barked. 'You'd better move yourself, girl, or you'll be squashed.' He raised his baton menacingly over the roof of the shanty.

Daisy couldn't think straight. She just stared at the policemen. Could things get any worse?

'Hang on, Bill,' said the second policeman – a short fellow with bright red hair. 'She's scared out of her wits.'

'Bloody gutter urchin. Her parents probably told her to stay here to stop us knocking the place down,' the first policeman answered.

'I don't have any parents,' Daisy shouted, finally finding her voice. 'I don't have anyone!'

'No parents, eh? Well, you'd better come with us,' the short policeman said. 'Call me Bluey. We'll take you to Miss Dunham's place. She likes kids. She'll take care of you there.'

'Really?' Daisy said. 'Somewhere I can stay?'

'Sure,' Bluey said. 'They'll give you food and clothes and even send you to school.'

Daisy felt a wave of relief wash over her. So there was a safe place for her after all. Some kindly lady who takes in poor kids and looks after them until they get back on their feet, Daisy thought. Maybe she's a rich widow who loves children and couldn't have any of her own. Maybe she'll be like a fairy godmother with a glittering dress and a magic wand.

Bluey's firm hand on her shoulder put an end to her daydreams. He steered her through the mud and chaos. All around, the huts lay flattened in the mud and Daisy could hear children crying and women screaming, and the blows of the batons as they reduced the last shanties to rubble.

It's all so cruel, Daisy thought, her eyes filling with tears. These poor, poor people.

The policeman opened the door of a black police car and bundled her in. She was still hugging her biscuit tin to her chest.

My first car drive, Daisy thought as the policemen jumped in to the front seats and started the engine. She stared, fascinated, at the city waking from its slumber as they drove through the quiet streets. Soon the comforting rhythm of the drive and the sun's warm morning rays through the window had her nodding her head. She lay down on the seat and fell asleep.

3
At the Orphanage

IT seemed just minutes later that Bluey was shaking her from her slumber.

'Come on, girl,' he said. 'We're here.'

Daisy's head felt thick as she sat up and looked out the window at a huge brick mansion with a tall spire. 'Oh my goodness! A castle,' she whispered to herself. 'Look at all the windows – and the different peaks on the roof!'

The mansion stood in a magnificent sweeping garden with circular plant beds surrounded by neat paths. Oh, there's a pond! I wonder if they have tadpoles, Daisy thought.

Large pine trees stood like silent guards. Daisy noticed there were two more big houses on either side of the main house. They look quite grand, too. This Miss Dunham must take care of a lot of children.

'What part of Melbourne is this?' Daisy asked. 'I've never been anywhere so posh.'

'This is Brighton, love,' Bluey replied as he walked her up the stone steps and rang the bell.

A girl a few years older than Daisy with a pinched face opened the door. 'Yes?' she asked.

'Police business, miss. Fetch a Cottage Mother, would you?'

'Come in,' the girl said, letting them into a high-ceilinged hall with gleaming floorboards.

'Wait here,' Bluey said, pointing to a wooden bench. Daisy sat with her tin on her lap. She could hear the high-pitched wail of a baby. Sounds hungry, poor mite, Daisy thought.

'Right then,' Bluey said, striding back five minutes later. By his side was a plump woman in a starched white uniform. 'This is Miss Dunham. She'll help you get settled.'

Daisy looked at them both in confusion. 'Can you tell me what this place is exactly before I decide if I should stay?'

An angry flush spread across Miss Dunham's face and down onto her several chins. Wiry hairs sprouted from a mole on her cheek. 'Oh!' she spluttered. 'Lady Muck will be letting us know if she'd like to stay, will she?'

Bluey tousled Daisy's hair. 'This is the Melbourne Orphanage. They'll keep you here till you're old enough to get a job.'

'I can't stay here all that time!' Daisy cried, jumping up. 'My family won't know where I am, and Amelia won't be able to send letters, and I have to find a way to track Dad down and get Flora back from Aunty May, and ...'

'I thought you said you were an orphan.' Bluey rubbed his forehead in confusion.

'I'm not!' Daisy cried. Everything was

happening too fast and her mind was a jumble.

'Well, do you have somewhere I can take you, then?' Bluey asked. Daisy thought of Aunty May's threatening face and sadly shook her head. 'No,' she said quietly, 'but ...'

'No matter,' Miss Dunham cut her off. 'Most of the children here aren't orphans. Their parents bring them in because they can't afford to keep them, so you'll fit in nicely.'

'Can I leave when I find Dad?' Daisy asked, glancing wildly from Bluey to Miss Dunham.

'Oh you are a funny one, aren't you?' the woman said coldly. 'Thinking you can breeze in and out when it suits you.'

Daisy decided that the woman's eyes looked like two dark raisins squashed into a fruit bun.

'You'll stay here now, till you're about sixteen,' Bluey said. 'It's for the best, love. Anything could happen to you out there.'

Sixteen! Daisy was too dazed to speak. She'd been expecting a lovely old widow's home, not a prison with an evil warden. 'But I don't have to stay, do I?' she said in a weak voice, 'I can go and visit my sister when I want to, can't I?'

'Right, I've had enough of your nonsense.' Miss Dunham nodded at Bluey. 'Thank you, Officer, you may go – everything is in hand here.' With that, she motioned for Daisy to follow her, and waddled off down the corridor.

'Bye now, good luck.' Bluey pulled his helmet on, and flung open the front door. A bright stream of warm October sun filled the hall, then the door closed and the warmth and light were shut out again.

'Hurry up,' Miss Dunham said as Daisy grabbed her tin, her heart pounding.

They hurried through the main building and out into large grounds, where the smaller houses stood. Miss Dunham ushered Daisy inside a red-brick cottage and led her into a dormitory with fifteen metal beds in tight rows. Daisy could see that a small doorway led to a washroom, where a line of basins filled the wall. She wrinkled her nose at the strong chemical smell in the room.

Miss Dunham walked to a bank of steel lockers. She took a key from her pocket and unlocked the one at the end. 'You will be Number Ten. See? It's painted on the locker and stamped on these boots, and you will sew it into these clothes. They look about your size.'

She passed Daisy a neatly folded bundle. 'These are your school clothes and your day clothes. You are expected to take excellent care of them. You will sleep here,' she said and pointed to a bed against the wall. 'Now, take those clothes into the washroom and get changed. I'll have one of the other girls come and sort you out.' Miss Dunham left her alone in the dormitory.

Daisy quickly hid the tin under the bed and went to change. She slipped a long-sleeved dress over her head and did up the buttons with shaking fingers. It was tight around her neck and made her feel like she was choking. She ran her finger inside the collar and tried to loosen it. It felt strange to be wearing something clean after so long. She sat on a small bench to pull on the new boots. They were too big and flopped around on her feet. She saw that they had a number ten stamped on the bottom. I really am a prisoner, she thought sadly, letting her hair fall over her face to cover her tears. I don't even have a name anymore.

'Hello, new girl!' a bright voice called.

Daisy quickly wiped her face and looked up to see a small girl smiling at her.

'I'm Edith,' she said, skipping into the room to shake Daisy's hand. 'Ooh, it's something fearful to be the new girl, ain't it? How are you doing? What do you think of your clothes? Must be nice to be clean for a change. We'd best do something about that hair, though, before the Cottage Mother gives you a slap for looking like a right urchin.'

Daisy stared at Edith in fascination. She looked like a little pixie with crazy short hair and a pointy chin. My goodness, I've never heard anyone talk so much, Daisy thought.

Before she could answer, Edith was off again. 'So, you know this is the washroom, sure enough, and you've seen your bed. I'll show you the dining room when the gong goes and tomorrow you'll be at school with the rest of us.'

Daisy opened her mouth to answer, but she wasn't quick enough.

''Course I should be there now, but Miss Fielding needs help with the babies sometimes, so she pulled me out of class, not that I mind. What with all that maths and writing they make us do, it's good to give the brain a rest.'

She gave Daisy a broad, warm smile and Daisy couldn't help but feel a bit better.

'I'm Daisy,' she said. 'I shouldn't be here at all – it's all a dreadful mistake.' She burst into shuddering sobs. Edith wrapped her in a warm hug.

'Oh, it's all right, everyone cries when they first get here. It'll be grand in a few days. Well, maybe not grand, but good enough to get by.' She jumped up again and grabbed a brush from the shelf. 'Now, let's get that hair seen to. You're lucky you weren't here last night! We had the nit check – you can probably still smell the Lysol they put on our heads, can you?'

Daisy nodded as Edith pulled hard at her tangled hair, talking all the while as she brushed it, parted it and plaited it into two neat braids.

'There now, a spot of lunch and everything will feel brand new, won't it?'

Daisy nodded again slowly, but she couldn't imagine ever feeling better about this place.

'Well, we've got time for a bit of a tour before lunch, how does that sound?' Edith grabbed Daisy's hand. 'Me and you are in Cottage Four together,' she said, and led Daisy out the front door and into the grounds. 'And over there is Three – that's the toddlers – then there's Babies in One, and Six and Five are the boys.'

Daisy stepped out into the sunshine and tried to take in all the new information. 'It's all so big and grand,' she said.

'Yeah, well, you probably won't think it's all that fancy soon, that's for sure,' Edith said. 'Oh!' She pointed to a tall, narrow house behind them. 'I forgot Cottage Two – that's Day Girls.'

'What are Day Girls?' Daisy asked.

'When you get to fourteen or fifteen, you don't go to school no more, you just get to be a full-time slave to the orphanage.' She turned to give Daisy a grimace. 'Mostly the Day Girls run the kitchen and look after the little ones. They have to work awful hard, poor loves.

'My little brother, Freddy, is in Toddlers.' Edith's voice grew quieter. 'I don't see him much 'cos they keep the cottages separate, but sometimes I can play with him on the weekend

for a bit.' She led Daisy into a wide courtyard.
'See over there, that's the vegie garden – the
Backyard Boys look after that. And there's the
tool shed and the Infirmary – but don't bother
getting sick, they don't look after you at all.'

Daisy's head was spinning. This can't be
real! she thought. She tried squeezing her eyes
closed and opening them again.

'What's the matter with you?' Edith laughed.
'Got a twitch or something?'

Daisy sighed. It was real all right. 'No, just
something in my eye,' she answered.

'Ooh, look!' Edith suddenly exclaimed.
'The toddlers are out.' She dashed off to a
small playground, where a dozen little children
wandered around or sat quietly on the bare
ground. Edith put her hand through the wire
that surrounded the yard. 'Freddy, Freddy,' she
called, and a small blond boy looked around.

'Edie!' he cried, and toddled over to the wire
and grabbed Edith's hand.

'Oooh, you dribbly devil,' Edith laughed as he kissed her hand. 'This is my little brother,' she said, turning back to Daisy. 'He's only three. Isn't he a poppet?'

Daisy smiled at the little boy and he gave her a shy wave.

'Our ma and pa died when Freddy was just a tiny baby,' Edith explained, and reached her other arm through the wire to rumple Freddy's hair. 'They got the Consumption and died within a week of each other.'

Daisy wasn't sure what the Consumption was, but didn't like to ask. *So Edith is a proper orphan,* she realised. *She really has no one else but this little chap. I'm so lucky – I have Dad and Flora, and Amelia, and Elsie and Mabel, too, not that I'll probably ever see them again, now that I'm stuck here,* she thought gloomily.

She turned around to take in the large grounds and saw something that made her gasp. 'Oh my goodness! A horse!' she cried, and raced toward a small paddock.

Edith ran behind her after kissing Freddy goodbye. 'Oh yeah, I forgot to say, that's Hero. He pulls the plough and helps the Backyard Boys with garden chores.'

At the fence, Daisy held out her hand, talking gently to the brown Clydesdale. He wandered slowly over to her and nuzzled her fingers. Daisy hurriedly picked some fresh grass from her side of the fence and held it out. Her eyes pricked with tears as his warm breath tickled her hand. 'Good boy, good boy,' she said.

He twitched his ears in pleasure and Daisy saw her face reflected in his deep brown eyes.

'He likes you,' Edith said in surprise. 'He's a cantankerous old devil with most people.'

Daisy breathed in the familiar horsey scent and rubbed her cheek along his nose. She missed Jimmy so much it made her heart hurt.

'Hey, stop bothering the horse!' A short boy with wild curly hair came running up to them.

'What are you doing?' he demanded.

'Keep your knickers on, Harry,' Edith laughed. 'Hero seems to like this one.'

Daisy took a step back from the horse and stared at the boy. 'He's beautiful,' she said and smiled happily. 'How old is he?'

Harry moved past her to talk to the horse. 'You all right, fella?'

The horse whinnied quietly with pleasure and nuzzled into Harry's chest.

He turned to face Daisy. 'He's eighteen, since you asked, and he doesn't like being bothered by a bunch of annoying little kids who think it's fun to poke him with sticks and pull his mane.'

'Oh, no . . . I'd never . . .' Daisy stuttered.

'Yeah, well, just make sure you don't.' Harry glared. 'You shouldn't even be over here.'

'Oh, eat my hat, Harry,' Edith said and poked her tongue out at him. 'C'mon Daisy, it's almost lunchtime anyway and Dunham will be on the warpath if we get there late.' Edith tried to grab

Daisy's arm and drag her toward Cottage Four, but Daisy shook her off.

She moved toward Hero again and held out her hand, whispering gently under her breath. The horse moved away from Harry and came to her, gently butting his head against her shoulder.

Harry whistled softly. 'Well, I'll be,' he said.

'I would never hurt an animal,' Daisy said, looking at Harry intently. 'I have a horse at home. His name is Jimmy. I think he'd like you a lot.'

Harry gave her a grin, and Daisy noticed the riot of freckles across his cheeks. 'Okay then, new girl, you can pat Hero sometimes, but I'll be watching closely,' he said.

A bell rang from inside the main building.

'That's lunch,' Edith said. 'Come on, Daisy, we'll have to run.'

4

Frightening News

DAISY hungrily finished her porridge and slurped down the half cup of milk in front of her. It was sour and warm, but she knew there'd be nothing else till lunch.

She looked down the long table at the other children as they ate breakfast. After two weeks, she'd come to know them pretty well. She knew that Molly was always the top of the class, that Eunice was Miss Dunham's pet and always got out of scrubbing the floors. She knew that Doreen always looked pale and never spoke. Most importantly, she knew who to trust.

Daisy glanced at Edith, who gave her a sly wink from the other end of the table. Daisy smiled back. Edith's the only good thing about this place, she thought. Well, her and Miss Winston. Daisy thought about the kind teacher from their small school next door. Ooh – that reminds me, I must take back Miss Winston's book. She'll get in such trouble if Miss Dunham finds out she let me sneak it back to read in bed.

Apart from Edith and school, the orphanage was a horrible place. Sure, it was good to have food and a bed to sleep in, but knowing that she couldn't leave and that no one had a clue where she was made Daisy feel sick inside.

At night, as she lay on her itchy, straw-filled mattress, she thought about Dad and Flora. Were they together now, and looking for her? What about Elsie and Mabel? They must be so worried. And Amelia too. She must wonder why I've stopped writing. I hope she'll still want to be my best friend, Daisy thought sadly.

Sometimes she daydreamed about riding Jimmy, but it made her feel so wretched that she had to force herself to stop. At least she was able to visit Hero most days. Sometimes Harry let her help brush him down after a day's work.

Miss Dunham stalked up and down the table, keeping a close eye on them as they ate breakfast. She had a cruel, hard mouth and kept a thick wooden ruler in her pocket to swipe at any girl who dared even look the wrong way. But what Daisy hated most was Miss Dunham's hair. It looked as if she'd never washed it, only kept it in the same bun her whole life. I bet there are spiders living under there, Daisy thought with a shiver. Spinning webs. *Disgusting*.

As the last girl put down her spoon, Miss Dunham gave the command for them to stand behind their chairs. She inspected the empty bowls to make sure no food had been left and then ordered the girls to form two neat rows and file into the bathroom to wash.

Daisy managed to get a spot beside Edith. 'Is it Visiting Day again today?' she whispered, looking over her shoulder. She'd already been caught talking a few times, and didn't want to risk another rap on the knuckles.

''Fraid so,' Edith said glumly. 'Straight after church. Waste of a day if you ask me.'

Daisy nodded in agreement, as she noticed Doreen across the room, looking miserable. 'Why does Doreen always look so sullen?'

'She didn't use to,' Edith said under her breath, keeping her eyes on the sink. 'She was jolly good fun. But then her little sisters got adopted. She hasn't said boo to a goose since.'

Daisy's mouth dropped open, but Miss Dunham had stomped back into the room, so she said nothing, just quickly splashed cold water on her face. How could the orphanage break up a family like that?

Once they were in their room, Daisy turned

to Edith. 'How can sisters be separated?' she said. 'It's not fair! Can anyone just come here and take a kid away?'

'Look, it's dreadful but it happens all the time. Doreen has taken it harder than most kids do.' Edith paused and patted Daisy's arm. 'Remember, we orphans don't have any rights.'

'But ...' Daisy interrupted.

'I know, I know, you ain't a proper orphan,' she said, and gave Daisy a tight smile. 'But as far as the government reckons, we all are, and they can do what they like with us.'

'That's rotten,' Daisy said, angrily.

'Line up for church,' Miss Dunham yelled as she came into the room.

There's no way I'd let anyone adopt me, Daisy thought as she stood in line.

Two hours later, church was over and they were sitting on the uncomfortable wooden benches in the front hall for Visiting Day. Daisy looked around at the other children, dressed in their best clothes and forced to sit here every Sunday, waiting for family that never came. It's just cruel, Daisy thought angrily, getting the little kids' hopes up that a relative might come. Edith had told her that visitors were rare, but the younger children still looked up hopefully every time the door opened.

By day's end some of the them were in tears. Others looked so confused that Daisy wanted to hug them. Imagine if that was Flora, hoping that Dad or I might come. Her thoughts were interrupted by a violent volley of knocks. Miss Dunham stalked toward the door and pulled it open. Two girls stood in the sunlight.

'Mabel! Elsie!' Daisy cried with joy, and leapt off the bench to run towards her friends.

Miss Dunham swung around to face Daisy, her lips curling back like an angry bulldog's. 'Sit down!' she bellowed.

'Well, I never! That's a fine way to speak to our friend, isn't it Mabel?'

'It certainly is,' Elsie replied as the pair swept through the door. 'And her descended from royalty and everything.'

Miss Dunham's eyes flashed with interest for a second, then she gave herself a shake. 'Royalty my foot. She's as common as muck, that one. Now what would the likes of you be wanting with Daisy Sanderson, anyway?'

'We heard,' Mabel said, and pulled a bag of boiled lollies from her pocket, 'that it was Visiting Day.' She threw the sweets to her sister.

'So we decided,' Elsie continued, as she waved the sweets in Miss Dunham's face, 'to visit.'

'Well . . .' Miss Dunham blustered.

'Yes, very well, thanks,' Mabel said, and gave the confused woman a deep curtsey.

'Right then, Daisy, perhaps you could take us for a turn around the grounds,' Elsie said as she and Mabel swept past Miss Dunham and rushed to hug Daisy.

'You have one hour,' Miss Dunham yelled after them as they skipped down the hall.

Daisy gave Edith a smile as they passed. I wish she could come, too, she thought sadly.

'Oh my goodness, how did you find me?' she demanded as they burst into the yard. 'How's Flora? Does she know I'm here? Is she okay?'

'Hold your horses, country girl, you're going to burst your boiler,' Mabel said and untangled herself from Daisy's tight hug.

'Old Mrs Owens told us the coppers had taken you,' Elsie said. 'We thought they might bring you here. We came the next day, but they told us we had to come back on a Sunday.'

'Ma kept us home all last weekend doing chores, or we would have come sooner,' Mabel continued. 'We haven't said anything to Flora because we weren't even sure you were here till now.' She gave one of Daisy's plaits a gentle tug. 'Never seen you so posh before,' she laughed.

Daisy groaned. 'They make us put on good clothes in case people come and visit,' she said. 'But there's one good thing. Come and meet Hero.' Daisy led the way to the paddock, pointing out the cottages as they went. 'Here, boy,' she called. Hero wandered over slowly and nuzzled her neck. 'So Flora doesn't know where I am?' she asked.

'Well, that's partly why we're here,' Elsie said, and she stepped closer to take Daisy's hand.

'Your aunt's been boasting up and down the street that she's going to send Flora away to Sydney next month, I'm afraid,' Mabel said as she put an arm around Daisy's shoulder.

'Send her away? What do you mean?' Daisy cried. She pushed away from the girls and stood facing them, her hands on her hips. 'Where would she live? Who would take care of her?' She thought for a minute she might be sick.

Behind her, Hero whinnied gently and tossed his head but Daisy ignored him.

'It's a boarding school,' Mabel said. 'Turns out your aunt knows some old biddy who works in a posh school in Sydney. Flora's going to live with her and go to her school.'

'They jumped at the chance to have her,' Elsie said. She kicked at the ground miserably.

'But . . . but what does Flora think? How will she even get there? What if she gets lost?' A thousand questions crowded into Daisy's head.

'Come and sit down,' Mabel said, pulling Daisy to a patch of grass. 'You look awful pale.'

Daisy put her head on her knees.

'We told Flora that you was living down at Dudley Flats,' Elsie said. 'We've been pretending to bring messages from you.' Her face coloured a deep red. 'I hope that's okay.'

Daisy looked at Elsie's worried face and felt a surge of gratitude. 'Of course it's all right,' she said quietly. 'It would have been terrible if she thought I was missing. But what about Dad?' she asked. 'Has there still been no word?'

Elsie shook her head sadly. 'Sorry, Daisy.'

'Poor Flora,' said Daisy.

'She seems happy enough about the school,' Mabel said softly, and leant in to put her head next to Daisy's. 'Your aunt is going to travel up there on the train with her just after Christmas.'

'I can't let her go. It's too far. I'll never see her again!' Daisy said. 'Aunt May will never tell me where she is. I have to stop them, but what can I do while I'm stuck in here?'

'They really won't let you out?' Mabel asked.

Daisy shook her head. 'Not until I'm sixteen.' She leapt up from the ground and wiped her sleeve across her face. 'But I'm going to find a way to escape,' she cried. 'I'll *force* Aunty May to let Flora come with me – I'll tell her I'll go to the coppers and have her charged with kidnapping if she doesn't! Then we'll go on the track to find Dad. We'll pack some supplies, and go back to the farm and get Jimmy. I should have done that ages ago.'

'Good plan, country girl,' Elsie said, flinging her arms around Daisy's neck.

'Oof, careful,' Daisy laughed.

A bell rang from inside the orphanage, announcing the end of visiting time.

Mabel looked at Daisy with concern. 'Are you all right in here, then?'

Daisy grimaced. 'It's good to not be half-starved all the time, but knowing they want to lock me up for years, well . . .' She shivered.

A Day Girl appeared in the yard. 'You two have to leave now,' she called to the twins.

'Right then, we'll be off,' Elsie said. 'But we'll come again before too long.'

'Come *on*,' the Day Girl called impatiently, 'I'll be the one who gets it if you're not out of here in two minutes.'

The twins rushed off. Daisy was longing to talk to Edith, but when she got back to the cottage, Miss Dunham kept her busy with chores until bedtime.

As she climbed into bed, Daisy felt more tired than she could ever remember feeling. She pulled the itchy sheet up to her chin and wriggled around to find a comfortable spot on the straw mattress. A golden crack of summer sunshine peeked in at the bottom of the blinds.

If I was on the farm, Amelia and I would still be out catching tadpoles or picking strawberries, Daisy thought. But that life just seems like a dream now. She sighed and turned over. How on earth can I escape? she wondered. Maybe I could make a run for it on Visiting Day and just keep running until I get to Gertrude Street? The idea of sprinting out of the orphanage gates made her smile.

All around she could hear the slow, even breathing of the other girls, and an occasional snuffle or cough as they slept. The room smelt of disinfectant and sweaty boots. Daisy burrowed further into her mattress and within minutes she was asleep.

5
Harry's Plan

IN the morning, Edith wasn't in her bed and didn't line up with the other children to march to school. I wonder where she's got to, Daisy thought.

It wasn't until afternoon break, when the children flooded into the small schoolyard, that Edith finally came stumbling through the gate.

'Where have you been?' Daisy asked. She noticed dark circles under Edith's eyes. 'You look exhausted.'

'Oh, I'm all right. It's just been a hectic night and morning with the babies,' Edith said.

'They've got a measles outbreak in the baby cottage so a Day Girl came and woke me and got me to pitch in with the poor little devils. I never saw so many spots in all my life, I swear.'

Daisy laughed and pulled Edith to sit under a tree in a quiet corner of the yard so she could fill her in on all the news about Flora.

Edith gave a low whistle when Daisy was finished. 'That's a right to-do for sure. So tell me again what you reckon happened to your dad?' she said, chewing on a piece of grass.

'That's just the problem. I can't think for the life of me why he hasn't written, but I know he'd never just go away and leave us,' Daisy said.

'It's a bit of a mystery then, eh?' Edith said. 'At least I know for sure my ma and pa aren't ever coming back.' She looked up at the sky. 'But I reckon they're probably watchin' me from heaven. What do you think?'

'I'm sure they are,' Daisy said and gave Edith's arm a squeeze. 'The thing is, I have to find a way to escape and stop my aunt sending Flora away.'

'Well,' Edith said, sitting up and dusting off her dress, 'we're going to need a plan, aren't we? And you know who's a whizz with plans?'

'Who?' Daisy asked, a tiny feeling of hope creeping into her heart.

'Harry!' Edith said triumphantly.

'Really?' Daisy asked, twisting one plait around her finger. 'But why would he help us?'

'Don't worry about that,' said Edith with a wink, 'he owes me one.'

Imagine if he could help! Daisy thought. I could maybe be free by tomorrow.

'Ooh, and did you see Dunham's hair this morning?' Edith said. 'It was even more of a rat's nest than normal!'

Daisy giggled as the bell rang.

'Now, children,' Miss Winston, began once they were seated. 'We have just enough time for a story. Make yourselves comfortable.' She took a large book from the shelf behind her.

This is my favourite part of school, Daisy thought happily as she leant back in her desk. I wish we could stay here all day.

'Once upon a time,' Miss Winston read in her gentle voice. And soon Daisy was transported to a world where every story ended happily ever after.

After school, Daisy and Edith lined up to go back to the orphanage.

'What are you on today?' Edith whispered.

'The kitchen,' Daisy whispered back.

Edith gave her a sympathetic look as they filed back through the gate. 'With any luck we should be able to have a natter with Harry in the playroom after dinner,' she said.

The girls went to their cottage and changed into their day clothes.

'Can you steal five minutes to come and visit Freddy with me?' Edith asked as she buttoned her pinafore. 'He does love it so when he gets visitors.' She gave Daisy a hopeful smile.

'Of course,' Daisy said. 'If we're quick.'

The girls linked arms and rushed to the Toddler's Cottage. Edith knocked on the front door, and Ruby, a Day Girl opened it, a toddler on each hip. 'Come in, come in, Edith,' she said with a sigh. 'It's all hands on deck today.'

Daisy followed Edith into the cottage and screwed up her nose as a strong smell of wet nappies filled the air. At first, they couldn't see Freddy anywhere – he wasn't down on the floor or in one of the metal cots.

Eventually Daisy spotted him whimpering in a corner. 'There he is,' she said.

Edith gasped. She leapt over a small group of children playing blocks, pushed past Ruby and scooped Freddy up in her arms. 'Oh my poor baby, it's okay, Edie's here now,' she crooned as she rocked him and covered his face with kisses.

The little boy wrapped his plump arms

tightly around her neck and snuggled in close. After a few minutes he gave a happy sigh, popped a thumb in his mouth and fell asleep.

'Poor little thing was tired,' Daisy said, walking over to stroke Freddy's head.

'They should take better care of him,' Edith said, her eyes flashing angrily. 'I'll be having a word before I leave. Poor little mite only needed a cuddle.' She pulled Freddy in tight. 'I'm going to stay here a bit longer.'

'Okay,' Daisy answered, feeling a lump in her throat as she thought of Flora cuddled up to her. 'I'd better get to my chores.'

'Well, here you are at last,' Miss Dunham said as Daisy entered the kitchen. Esme and Gladys from her cottage were there already. 'I thought I'd be peeling potatoes myself, you took so long.' She pointed to a wide bench at the end of the room, where several large sacks of potatoes sat. 'Off you go, then. When you're finished come and see me. There's plenty more.'

Daisy tied on an apron, and took a small knife from one of the wooden drawers. She pulled up a stool beside the other girls.

'Kitchen is the worst job, I reckon,' Gladys said quietly, looking around to make sure Miss Dunham had left.

'But it's better than the washroom,' Daisy answered, plunging a potato into a tub of water.

'S'pose so, but at least there you can talk and no one catches ya,' Gladys said.

'I'd rather work out in the garden,' Daisy said, 'out in the sunshine. It's getting so warm now, you can feel summer in the air.'

'That's a boy's job, though,' Esme said. 'You're better off learning stuff that will help you run your own house one day.'

Daisy sighed. She couldn't imagine ever having her own house. It's all such a mess, she thought, shaking her head. She only had a few weeks to stop Aunty May from sending Flora to Sydney. She still had no idea where Dad was, and now he'd have no way to contact her. And how would she ever take Flora from Aunty May? But first she had to get out of this prison.

Daisy stared at the grubby potato in her hand. Harry was her last chance.

After a dinner of bread and jam, Edith and Daisy went to the playroom to look for Harry. He was in a corner poring over a newspaper, silently mouthing the words to himself.

'Watcha reading?' Edith demanded.

'None of your business,' Harry answered.

Daisy peered down at the page. There was a photo of a racehorse, his trainer holding his reins and smiling broadly. 'What a wonderful-looking horse!'

Harry looked up at her warily. ''Course he's wonderful. That's Phar Lap, the most magnificent racehorse in the world.'

'Oh yes,' Daisy said. 'My dad told me about

him, but I've never seen a picture. He's so tall, he must be fifteen hands high.'

'Seventeen to be exact,' Harry said proudly. 'Won almost every race he's been in for the past two years, and he'll be in the Cup next month.'

'The Melbourne Cup?' Daisy asked.

Harry nodded. 'Most famous horse race in all the country, and Phar Lap's gonna win it easily.' He took a deep breath and lowered his voice. 'And I'm gonna be there to see it.'

'But how?' Daisy asked.

'I have my ways,' Harry said mysteriously.

Edith moved closer and whispered to him, 'Well then, it couldn't be more perfect, could it? 'Cos Daisy needs to get out of here, too!'

Harry flicked his eyes up at Daisy and she could see him carefully weighing up the idea.

'But what about you, Edith? Don't you want to escape, too?' Daisy asked.

Edith shook her head. 'I need to stay here for Freddy. I got me own plans. In a couple of years

I'll be able to leave and get a job, and then I'm going to get Freddy out and take care of him.'

There was a burst of noise behind them from a group of children playing Snap.

'So come on, Harry, fess up and tell us your grand plan,' Edith said, poking him in the back.

'Well ...' Harry scanned the room to make sure no Cottage Mothers were around. 'You know how the cobbler comes on Tuesdays?'

Edith and Daisy nodded.

'Well, the Cup is on a Tuesday, so I reckon I'll climb into his cart, hide under some old blankets and sneak a lift back to the city.'

Daisy and Edith exchanged excited glances.

'He always leaves by noon and the race isn't till three, so there'd be time to get to the track and see Phar Lap romp home.' Harry crossed his arms and looked up at them, eyes shining.

'That's a *wonderful* idea. Could I ...?' Daisy hardly dared to hope that Harry might let her be part of his plan. We'll be like convicts escaping from prison! she thought.

'Well, I dunno,' Harry said, scratching his nose. 'Girls tend to muck everything up by getting all scared and hysterical.'

Edith punched Harry's arm. 'What a lot of tosh,' she said. 'Daisy is as brave and clever as any boy – you'd be lucky to have her along.'

Daisy nodded and chewed on the end of her plait as she imagined it. Harry *had* to say yes.

'Daisy Sanderson,' a voice thundered from the other side of the room. 'Did you not get enough dinner?'

Daisy's stomach lurched. 'Err ... yes ... Miss Dunham,' she said, turning around tentatively to face the angry Cottage Mother.

'Then why, pray tell, do you find it necessary to chew on your hair in such a disgusting manner?' the woman demanded. She stood over Daisy and tapped her ruler menacingly against one palm. 'Maybe we need to give you a haircut like we did for Miss Edith there?'

Daisy stared at her friend in horror. That's why her hair was so short and scruffy! That evil woman had chopped it all off. Edith ran a hand over her shorn head and looked down.

Mean old crow, Daisy thought, and pulled back her shoulders to stare Miss Dunham directly in the face. 'I'd be happy to have such a fashionable haircut as Edith's,' she said, her voice only shaking slightly. 'It's very pretty.'

Edith shot her a grateful look.

'Besides,' said Daisy thoughtfully, 'it would be so much easier than having to deal with a tangled head of hair every day, don't you think?'

A small wave of giggles broke out around her as the children stared at the messy lump of hair on Miss Dunham's head.

'Well, I never!' Miss Dunham turned and stamped out of the room in anger.

Daisy winked at Edith as the bell rang. Harry looked from one girl to the other. 'Okay,' he said as he gathered up the paper. 'You're in.'

6
An Eventful Day

THE morning bell clanged loudly through the dormitory and Daisy could hear the groans and sighs of the girls around her as they dragged themselves out of their warm beds.

'Come on, get moving,' Miss Dunham's dull voice echoed through the room. 'Those chores won't do themselves, you know.' She moved through the room rapping on the ends of the metal beds with her heavy ruler.

Daisy yawned and sat up. The floorboards were cold beneath her bare feet. She ran to the washroom and then to her locker to get dressed. The routines of the orphanage were familiar to her now and she knew she had to be fast. Quick, quick, she thought to herself as she pulled on her boots and ran back to her bed to frantically pull the covers smooth and tuck the ugly brown blanket tightly into the corners.

'Time's up,' Miss Dunham bellowed, and each girl hastily stood at the end of her bed, waiting to be inspected.

'Too sloppy. Do it again or miss breakfast!' Miss Dunham said, ripping the blanket off Molly Carter's bed.

Mean old hag, Daisy thought, and shot Molly a sympathetic look.

'Did you even wash?' Miss Dunham sneered, peering into the scared face of Lucy O'Connor, who could only nod her head in response.

'I doubt it. Do it again!'

As she drew closer, Daisy crossed her fingers behind her back for good luck.

'Nails!' Miss Dunham demanded, stopping

in front of Daisy.

Daisy immediately held out her hands.

'Teeth!'

Daisy opened her mouth wide.

'Humph,' Miss Dunham answered and, unable to find any faults, began to walk away. Thank goodness, Daisy thought with relief.

But then the woman stopped. She stared at the floor and pointed with her ruler. 'What's this?' she asked, kicking Daisy's biscuit tin from under the bed.

'That's mine,' Daisy said. 'It's got my personal things in it.'

'Give it to me,' Miss Dunham ordered.

Daisy felt her breath quicken as she bent to pick the tin up. She held it tightly to her chest.

'I said hand it over,' Miss Dunham thundered, and Daisy reluctantly passed her the tin.

Miss Dunham pulled the lid open roughly and Amelia's letters spilled onto the floor. Daisy went to pick them up.

'Leave them! Oh, look girls,' the woman said in a taunting voice, 'a photograph of a horsey ... Oh and here, look, it's a bit of horse hair. I wouldn't be surprised if that were a health hazard.'

Daisy looked over at Edith, whose eyes were shiny with anger. She looks like she's going to explode, Daisy thought as she watched the colour rising in Edith's cheeks.

'I'll be taking this with me,' Miss Dunham said, tucking the tin under her arm.

'No!' Daisy cried and reached out to take the tin back.

'Hands *off.*' Miss Dunham gave Daisy's fingers a sharp whack with the ruler.

Daisy pulled her hand back in pain, her fingers already turning blue from the blow.

'Now you.' Miss Dunham pointed at Molly. 'Pick up all this rubbish on the floor and take it to the Backyard Boys to put in the incinerator.'

Daisy covered her mouth with her hands as

tears poured down her face.

Molly gave Daisy a sad look as she gathered the letters and left the room with them.

'And you,' Miss Dunham said, pointing her ruler in Daisy's face. 'You can forget about breakfast. Get the bucket and scrubbing brush and make that washroom floor gleam. Maybe that will teach you a lesson for hiding things.' With that, she lumbered out of the room.

Daisy's thoughts were reeling. They were the last bits of home I had. Now I have nothing. Nothing at all. She put her fingers in her mouth.

'Daisy, I'm so sorry.' Edith's wiry arms were around her in seconds. 'That nasty old hag needs to be taught a lesson,' she said. 'She was cross 'cos of what you said about her hair in the playroom.'

Daisy nodded. 'I know, but they were the only things I had from home,' she gulped, trying hard to swallow her tears. 'I feel like I'm starting to disappear, Edith. Maybe Dad and

Flora and Jimmy have forgotten me by now anyway. Maybe I should just forget about them, like Miss Dunham says.'

'Don't you dare!' Edith grabbed Daisy's hand.

'Ow,' Daisy said, pulling back her injured fingers.

'Oops, sorry,' Edith said, 'but look, Daisy, you can't give up. You have to be strong. We'll find a way to get you back to your family.'

Daisy sighed. 'I hope so,' she said softly.

'And what's more, we'll find a way to get back at that wicked old Dunham, too,' Edith said, balling her hands into fists. 'We'll make her pay, Daisy. You mark my words.'

'Daisy, psst . . . Daisy, come here.'

Daisy looked up from mopping the kitchen floor. She arched her back to try to ease some of the stiffness and looked around to see Edith hiding behind one of the benches. 'What are you doing?' she laughed.

Edith held her finger to her lips and pointed at Miss Dunham, who stood just outside the door tapping her ruler on her hand. She stepped into the room and swept her eyes over the benches and floor. 'You've missed a spot in the corner,' she barked at Daisy. 'Mind you get all those pots finished by bedtime, Molly,' she said to the girl at the sink, then shuffled out of the room again.

Edith popped out from behind the bench again. 'Phew,' she laughed, 'that was close. Just pretend I'm a ghost and you never saw me.' Edith rushed over to the large pantry in the corner and checked over her shoulder to make sure there were no Cottage Mothers around, then opened the door and started rummaging inside.

Daisy watched curiously as her friend searched through bags of flour and sugar.

'Aha!' Edith finally said triumphantly. She

took a small paper bag from her pocket and spooned in some white powder.

'Are you going to make a cake in bed tonight?' Daisy asked.

'Maybe she wants to cook up a batch of scones for a midnight feast?' Molly suggested, and the girls giggled.

'Never you mind,' Edith said, tapping her finger against her nose. 'The less you know, the more fun it will be, I promise.' With a cheeky grin, she ran from the room.

'That Edith,' Molly said, turning back to the pile of pots in the sink, 'always up to something. At least she makes life interesting.'

Thank goodness for Edith, Daisy thought. The longer I'm here, the more I feel like a criminal in a gaol with no hope of ever leaving.

Two hours later, Daisy was tucked up in bed and almost asleep when an ear-splitting scream filled the air and a figure in a long white nightgown burst into the dormitory. One of the older girls ran to light the gas lamp, and suddenly there was Miss Dunham, barefoot with disheveled hair and white foam surging from her mouth, screeching loudly,

Several of the girls shrieked with fear.

'It's tetanus, she's got the tetanus!' one cried.

'No, she's gone mental,' another called.

Daisy looked over and noticed Edith running in with Freddy wrapped around her in a tight hug. She jumped into bed and snuggled his little body close to her.

What on earth was going on? Daisy slipped out of bed to find out. 'What have you done?' she whispered to Edith as Miss Dunham cried out and rubbed at her foaming mouth.

'Oh, it's nothing really.' Edith grinned at her. 'Just a bit of bicarb soda in place of her tooth powder. Works a treat, don't you think? And it created a handy distraction so I could sneak

Freddy in to bed with me.'

Daisy couldn't help but giggle. 'But Edith, if she finds Freddy here she'll hang you.'

'I think she's a bit preoccupied for that, don't you?' Edith gently stroked Freddy's cheek. 'I just couldn't leave him alone one more night, Daisy,' she said softly. 'I'll sneak him back in the morning before anyone notices.'

Daisy nodded and patted Edith's shoulder. She's the bravest person I know, she thought as she returned to her own bed.

Miss Dunham finally stopped screaming as the foam started to dissolve, and went back in her room, where she could be heard noisily washing out her mouth and spitting into her basin. 'Quiet!' she yelled between mouthfuls. 'Anyone not in bed will meet my ruler.'

The girls scrambled back to their beds and soon Daisy could hear the sound of quiet breathing all around her. What a lovely night, she thought happily as she drifted off to sleep.

7

A Terrible Loss

DAISY kicked her feet against the legs of the hard bench and yawned loudly.

'Daisy Sanderson!' a voice called. 'Do sit up straight and stop fidgeting, will you?'

Daisy looked up to see Miss McCracken from the Toddler's Cottage pointing at her. She pulled herself up straight on the bench and tried to invent a story to keep herself amused while Visiting Day dragged on.

I'll pretend I'm a princess locked high in a castle tower, just waiting to be rescued, Daisy thought. But somehow the idea of waiting for someone to save her seemed far too dull. I'd rather save myself, she thought. She hadn't had a chance to talk to Harry again, but she hoped to find him this afternoon. It was nine days now till the Cup and they needed to make plans. That's if this dreadful morning ever ends, she thought. I wonder what Mabel and Elsie are doing right now? The twins hadn't been back to visit, and Daisy was desperate for news.

A knock at the front door made the children turn their heads to watch as a well-dressed young couple was ushered in to the Superintendent's office. Daisy had only seen Mr Geoffery, the Superintendent, at church when he handed out threepences for the children to put on the collection plate. He seemed a cross old man who had little time for the children whose lives he controlled.

Daisy raised her eyebrows at Edith. This looks interesting, she thought.

After ten minutes, the couple came out of

the office again, smiling and shaking hands with Mr Geoffery.

'Adoption,' Edith whispered.

Before Daisy could answer, Miss Dunham appeared with one of the Day Girls, who was carrying a small child. She handed the young boy to the woman. Daisy felt Edith go stiff beside her. Suddenly her friend shot up and raced down the hall.

'No,' she screamed. 'You can't! Not Freddy!'

Daisy felt sick to her stomach. The couple was here to take Edith's little brother away.

Miss McCracken ran after Edith and grabbed her around the waist as Mr Geoffery ushered the couple out the front door.

'Edie, Edie,' Freddy called plaintively.

'Don't take him – *please*!' Edith screamed.

But Mr Geoffery just slammed the door, and Freddy was gone. The rest of the children broke into startled whispers. Edith collapsed on the floor and Daisy ran to comfort her.

'Freddy,' Edith sobbed. 'Freddy.'

'How ridiculous!' Miss McCracken said, pulling Edith to her feet.

'Leave her alone,' Daisy cried, and got a stinging slap on the face that almost knocked her over.

'Take her to the dormitory and both of you get changed into your day clothes,' Miss Dunham ordered. 'The best thing you can do is forget that you had a brother,' she said to Edith.

Daisy looked at the women in disgust. That's *it*, she thought to herself. I'm getting out of this place as soon as I can.

That afternoon, Daisy and Edith sat beneath a big tree in the back garden.

'I'm coming with you, Daisy,' said Edith. 'I have to find Freddy. I can't just let them take him away like that. I can't bear it.'

'But where will you look? How will you

find him?' Daisy asked. 'The city's so big.'

'I don't know,' Edith admitted, silent tears dripping off the end of her nose and into her lap. 'I just know I have to try.'

'Right then.' Daisy stood up to wipe the grass from her dress. 'We need to find Harry and work out a grand plan.' She turned to give Edith an encouraging smile. 'Then we can both be back with the people we love.'

Daisy linked her arm in Edith's as they walked towards Hero's paddock, where Harry was leaning over the fence feeding him a handful of grass.

He looked up as the girls approached. 'Sorry about Freddy,' he said quietly to Edith, who just nodded in response.

'We're here about the escape. Edith's coming, too, now,' Daisy said, stepping forward to pat Hero's nose. 'So tell us the plan.'

'Both?' Harry looked confused for a second. 'Well, righto. Old Mac the cobbler will be here next Tuesday at eight. He leaves at exactly twelve 'cos his wife likes him to be home for lunch.' He leant to tear out another clump of grass. 'That gives us plenty of time to get into his cart, hide under some old sacks, and get to the city in time for the Cup.'

'But isn't it a long way from the city to the race track?' Edith said, wrinkling her forehead. 'How will you get all the way there in time?'

'Don't you worry about that. I know a way,' Daisy said, and gave Harry a thumbs-up.

'But you don't need to come to the race, Daisy. Don't you want to go straight to your aunt's?' he said.

'That's okay,' Daisy said with a shrug. 'The least I can do is help you get to the racecourse.'

'Thanks,' Harry mumbled, dipping his head.

'And you should stick with me, too, Edith,' Daisy said, putting an arm around her friend. 'We'll be better off together. If Dad's back, he can help you find Freddy. And Mabel and Elsie will know where to start.'

Edith nodded, and bit her lip as fresh tears rolled down her face.

'But how will we be able to sneak away from school to get to the cart?' Daisy asked, turning to Harry in dismay. 'I hadn't thought of that.'

Harry pulled Hero's head closer to him and muttered to the horse. 'Good thing us boys know what's goin' on, eh mate?'

'*Fine*,' Daisy snapped, waving a bunch of fresh grass over the fence, 'I guess I won't help you get to the racetrack, then.' Hero obediently trotted away from Harry to chomp at the grass Daisy offered.

'Fine, fine,' Harry laughed. 'You win.' He looked around to make sure they were alone. 'What I thought we should do is all pretend to be sick at school. Miss Winston will send us to the Infirmary. But instead we can sneak into the driveway and get into Mac's cart.'

Edith groaned. 'Miss Winston isn't stupid.

She's not going to believe we all suddenly got sick at the same time.'

Harry gave her a long look, but decided to ignore her angry tone. 'That's the second half of my plan,' he said. 'I managed to sneak a bottle of red ink from Miss Winston's desk yesterday. I reckon if we put red spots on our faces and then go to her one by one complaining of a headache, she'll be so worried about measles that she'll send us out of there in no time.'

Daisy clapped her hands with delight. 'I couldn't have come up with a better story myself,' she cried, slapping Harry on the back.

'What will happen if we're caught?' Edith asked, frowning.

'The cane, I guess,' said Daisy. 'And scrubbing the washroom for the rest of our lives. But imagine if we make it!'

'Well, I still think it's crazy,' said Edith, 'but I'm desperate enough to try.'

'All right.' Harry nodded. 'We're on.'

8
The Escape

TODAY'S the day, Daisy thought just over a week later as her stomach flip-flopped with excitement. Today I'll see Flora again, and maybe even Dad, and leave this prison forever.

She couldn't help but give a little skip of joy as the rows of children snaked around the orphanage grounds to the schoolyard.

'Oh Edith,' Daisy gasped, taking Edith's hands and swinging her around. 'Isn't it the most thrilling adventure ever?'

'Shhh,' Edith said and pulled away. 'We're supposed to be sick, remember?'

Daisy frowned. 'Sorry. I got carried away.'

'It's all right,' Edith said. 'Now, here.' She dragged Daisy away from the rest of the children to a quiet corner of the garden. 'I have the jar of ink from Harry, and we'll use a twig to put the spots on so we don't mess up our fingers.' She picked up a small stick from the ground and wiped it clean. 'I'll do you first.'

Daisy leaned in close as Edith dipped the end of the twig into the ink, shook it slightly, then pressed it gently onto Daisy's face.

'Ooh, it looks a treat,' Edith said. She dotted the ink across Daisy's face and onto her neck.

'It tickles,' Daisy said, and tried not to laugh.

'Right, now do me.' Edith handed Daisy the bottle and stick.

Daisy quickly repeated Edith's actions and soon her friend had a bad case of the measles.

'We'll have to keep our faces down until we're ready to go,' Edith said. 'And it will be best if we go one at a time. Harry said he'll watch the clock and go first, then I'll wait ten minutes and go after him,' said Edith. 'Then you come ten minutes after that.'

Daisy was too excited to speak, so she just nodded with delight.

'Let's go,' Edith said. 'I'll leave the ink here under the tree for Harry. Ooh look – he's over there glaring at us to hurry up already.'

In class, Daisy was careful to keep her head bent over her books. She didn't have to wait long before Harry got up from his seat and walked slowly to the front of the room. He's not a very good actor, Daisy thought. I should have given him some tips.

Harry stood before Miss Winston's desk and Daisy could see the teacher's look of alarm as she saw the spots on his face. Daisy grinned as Miss Winston handed Harry a note and he staggered from the room holding his head.

Terrible performance. Daisy sighed again, shaking her head. I can't wait for my turn.

She tapped her pencil on the edge of the desk impatiently. Edith frowned, and Daisy immediately turned back to her work.

A few minutes later, Edith put down her pen. She gave Daisy a quick wink and walked slowly up to Miss Winston's desk.

The teacher gave a jolt of alarm as she looked up at yet another spotty face. She scanned the class and noticed Daisy watching intently.

'Come to the front please, Daisy,' she said.

Oh no! I was supposed to be hiding my face, not gawking like a busy-body. Have I ruined everything? Daisy wondered.

'Yes, Miss Winston?'

'Daisy, dear, do you feel quite well?' the teacher asked kindly.

Daisy swapped worried glances with Edith.

'We-ell,' she said, 'I do have a terrible headache and my throat hurts, Miss.' Daisy folder her arms across her body and swayed slightly on the spot.

'Oh dear, that's what I was worried about,' Miss Winston said. 'You're covered in spots just like poor Edith here, and Harry Waller too.' She scanned the class once more. 'But it looks like it's just the three of you for now. You'd better get to the Infirmary quick sticks.' She scribbled a note and held it out, but just as Edith was about to take it, she pulled back.

'Goodness, what am I thinking?' she said. 'Of course I should walk you both over to the Infirmary myself. Why, Daisy, you look as if you might faint any minute,' she said.

Oh darn my acting skills, Daisy thought, her head a swirl of panic. If Miss Winston came with them they would be found out for sure.

'But Miss Winston,' Edith said, 'there will be no one to watch the class. I'm not feeling as poorly as Daisy. I can help her.'

'Oh yes,' Daisy added. 'I'll be as right as rain with Edith.' She smiled bravely.

'Well ...' Miss Winston tapped her fingers on

her teeth thoughtfully. 'I suppose if you're sure. Take this note to Matron. I do hope you will be better soon, girls.'

'Thank you,' they murmured, and left the classroom with Daisy leaning theatrically on Edith's arm. They walked quietly through the yard, too stunned to speak.

Finally Edith broke the silence. 'I can't believe it worked,' she said.

'And she was so lovely,' Daisy added. 'I feel dreadful for lying to her.'

'Me too,' Edith agreed. 'But it's for a good cause, remember.'

'It sure is,' Daisy agreed. 'I'll write to Miss Winston to apologise once I'm back home.'

Harry was waiting for them, kneeling down behind Old Mac's cart in the driveway. He was talking softly to the grey horse at the front. 'It's all right, girl,' Daisy heard him saying as they drew nearer. 'We're friends, we mean you no harm.' The horse whinnied happily as Harry stroked her flank.

He really is a natural, Daisy thought. No wonder he wants to see Phar Lap so badly.

'Did you take the long way here?' Harry asked, and gave them an annoyed look. 'I thought you must have chickened out.'

'Miss Winston almost decided to take us to the Infirmary herself,' Daisy whispered, and bobbed down behind the cart with Harry.

'You better get down too, Edith,' he ordered. 'Anyone could see you standing there.'

Edith hastily knelt beside Daisy.

'Okay, Edith, you go first. Just stay down until you're at the end of the cart, and for pity's sake make a fast job of climbing up and getting the sack on top of you,' Harry instructed.

'Oh, don't go getting all in a tizzy.' Edith made a face at Harry. 'I'm sure I can manage it.'

She quickly jumped up on to the cart and lay down, covering herself with a sack.

'Your go, Daisy,' Harry said.

Daisy took a deep breath to try to stop herself shaking. She snuck along the side of the cart, bent low. And then, with a quick scan of the grounds, she leapt onto the tray and threw herself down beside Edith. The sack was thick and hot and stank of boot polish, but Daisy covered herself and lay perfectly still.

In seconds, Harry was beside them. He pushed himself up and wriggled to the end of the cart closest to the horse. 'You okay there, girls?' he whispered.

'I would be if you'd only get your mucky boots out of my face,' Edith hissed back.

There was a crunch on the gravel and all three froze.

'Ah, there's me girl, sat waitin' for me like the angel she is.'

It's Old Mac, Daisy thought. We're free!

9
At the Races

A heavy box landed with a thud in the back of the cart, narrowly missing Edith's feet.

Daisy could hear Old Mac pull himself up onto the cart with a groan, and pick up the reins. The leather slapped against the horse's back, and they were off. Daisy found Edith's hand under the sacks and squeezed tight.

It was a long, bumpy ride in the cart, and Daisy felt sweat running down her face even though the day was overcast. She could only see tiny pinpricks of light coming through the sack. As they drew closer to the city, the roads became smoother and the sounds of traffic increased. Daisy's heart beat faster as she heard the clang of the trams in the distance.

'Woah, girl,' Old Mac called, and the cart came to a slow stop. 'Good work, my lovely. I'll be back with some water for you directly.'

'Quick,' Harry said. 'Before he comes back.'

Daisy threw the sack off with relief, and felt cool air on her hot face. She scrambled out of the cart with Edith and Harry, and they ran to the shelter of some nearby bushes.

'Urgh,' she said. 'That was so hot and smelly.'

'Awful,' Edith agreed. 'But we made it!' She threw her arms around Daisy.

'That's enough of the mushy stuff,' Harry said with scowl. 'We have to get moving. I have a horse race to get to. Here.' He passed them a damp handkerchief. 'Wipe your faces. There's metho on that to get the spots off.'

'Pooh, that stinks,' Daisy laughed, dabbing the cloth at Edith's ink measles. She felt giddy

with joy at being free. This must be how heroes
feel when they're released from dungeons, she
thought to herself. 'Let's walk that way,' Daisy
said after Edith had wiped all the spots off her
face. She pointed toward a group of shops.
'Then I'll be able to get my bearings.'

They hurried down the road. 'Oh, look,'
Daisy said. 'We're in luck! There's a tram stop
right there – oh, and there's Chinatown. We
can catch a tram from here and we should be at
the racetrack in a few minutes.'

'Except we don't have the dosh to pay for a
tram ride,' Harry sneered. 'I knew I shouldn't
have trusted a girl with a crucial part of the plan.
Now I'm going to miss Phar Lap after all.' He
pursed his lips angrily and strode away.

Daisy ran after him. 'It's okay, Harry,' she said.
'We don't need money – not to ride the trams
how my friends taught me.'

'Are you sure?' Harry asked hopefully.

''Course. Ooh, here comes one now! Just do

what I do.' Daisy crossed the road and waited for the tram to stop. As passengers spilled out, she looked for the conductor. Seeing him on the right side of the tram, she motioned to Edith and Harry to follow her to the left side.

'Right, just stand up here,' she said, jumping on the tram's running board, 'and hold on tight to this pole. Keep your heads down.'

Harry and Edith nervously stood behind Daisy as the driver rang the bell and the tram rumbled to life.

I'd forgotten how wonderful this feels, Daisy thought as the tram barrelled through the streets. It's like flying! 'This tram goes up Flemington Road, so I guess it must go straight to the racetrack,' she yelled.

'There it is,' Edith shrieked some time later. 'Look at all the people going in.'

'Get ready to jump off at the next stop,' Daisy called over the wind that was blowing her hair into her face. 'Remember to stay low.'

The tram shuddered to a halt almost directly in front of the racecourse. The area was abuzz with people arriving laden with picnic baskets and dressed in fancy clothes.

'That was super fun,' Harry cried as they ran to the side of the road. 'I've never been on a tram before, let alone on the side of one.'

'Really?' Daisy said, trying to smooth down her wind-blown hair. 'But you're a city kid! How could you not have been on a tram?'

Harry blushed. 'There aren't many trams at the orphanage, now, are there?' he said crossly and walked ahead of them.

Edith grabbed Daisy's arm. 'Don't mind him, Daisy, it's just that he's been in the orphanage since he was a baby. It's the only life he knows.'

'I didn't even think,' Daisy gasped.

'Just leave it,' Edith said. 'It's best that way.' She stood staring at the sea of people streaming into the gates of Flemington Racecourse. 'Did you ever see such glamour?'

Daisy shook her head in wonder as two women wearing long white furs sauntered past. What utterly divine hats, she thought, touching her scruffy hair again. I've never seen so many ribbons and feathers. How elegant.

'Come on,' Harry called impatiently. 'Would you ever stop gawking and get a move on.'

The girls ran to catch up with him.

'Right, now, all we need to do is sneak past the front gates and we're home,' Harry said.

'Well, *you* might be,' Daisy reminded him, 'but Edith and I have got family to find.'

Harry looked crestfallen. 'Oh go on,' he said, 'you're so close and it will be such a grand day. I reckon Phar Lap's gonna make history.'

'I don't know ...' Daisy said doubtfully. 'I really want to get to Gertrude Street.'

'But you'll be telling your grandchildren about this one day,' Harry said. He awkwardly stepped off the curb and almost fell in the gutter as a group of men in top hats pushed past him.

'Watch it there, Harry! It's busy out here in the real world,' Edith laughed.

Daisy looked at Harry's face and realised he was nervous. What would it be like to never have seen the world outside the orphanage? she wondered. It must be terrifying to be around so many people at once.

'Could we just see Harry's precious horse run, and then be off?' Edith asked.

'Well, all right,' Daisy agreed. 'But once the race is over we have to leave straight away.'

'Deal,' Edith said.

'Follow me,' said Harry with relief.

Edith and Daisy clasped hands and stayed close to Harry as he weaved through the tight crowd. There were ticket booths on opposite sides of the large metal gates at the entrance. Harry motioned for the girls to crouch down and sneak behind a large group of people as they bought their tickets and wandered into the racecourse.

Within minutes, they were through the

entrance and into the sweeping grounds.

It's all so beautiful, Daisy thought, looking across the lush green lawns that rolled down to the racetrack. A sea of people filled the huge lawn and the two large grandstands behind them.

At the sound of trumpets, the crowd surged toward the railing around the track and began cheering loudly as the horses began racing. A man called the race over a loudspeaker, firing out names quicker than Daisy could catch.

'Oh no – have we missed it?' she called.

'No,' Harry said. 'Big Red's not running till three. We've got plenty of time.'

'My head is spinning with all these people and this noise,' Edith said.

'We'll find a patch of grass and plant ourselves.' Harry led the way to a quieter spot near a big flower garden. 'Now, I want to go off and do a bit of poking around the stables, but I'll make sure I'm back before the big race.'

Daisy nodded. 'Will it be long?' she asked.

Inside she had begun to feel jumpy and anxious again. I'm so close to Flora now, she thought.

'Just another hour or so,' Harry said, and waved as he wandered off to find the stables.

Daisy leant back on her elbows to watch the crowd. I feel like I'm in a fairytale, she thought.

People sat on rugs all around them, eating lunch from picnic baskets. Daisy's stomach rumbled. It had been ages since breakfast.

'Be nice to have a bite of something,' Edith said and gave her a gentle nudge.

'I was just thinking the same thing,' Daisy replied. She licked her lips hungrily and looked over at a row of bins near the racecourse fence.

'Wait here,' she said to Edith. She walked past each bin slowly, and took a quick glance inside. The first two were filled with papers and empty bottles, but the third held a bulging brown paper bag. That looks promising, she thought. She quickly dipped her hand into the bin and swung the bag out. She looked around, but no one seemed to have noticed. She wandered along the bins a bit further. Ooh look – race program! Harry will like that. Underneath it was a half-empty bottle of lemonade. Right, let's be having you then, she thought, and thrust her hand in once more. She ran back to Edith with her treasures. 'A picnic!' She dropped to her knees and rustled the paper bag open. Inside sat a half-eaten sandwich.

'You're so clever,' Edith said.

'Why, thank you,' Daisy said, as she munched on her share of the sandwich, gazing at the fascinating people all around. I can't wait to tell Flora about it. She pulled dreamily at some blades of grass and suddenly caught sight of something shiny.

'Oh my goodness, look, Edith!' Daisy cried. 'It's a shilling, a whole big shining shilling just sitting in the grass waiting for us to find it.'

Edith gasped with delight. 'You're rich!'

'*We're* rich, more like it,' Daisy pulled Edith to

her feet. 'Come on, let's go and get an ice cream for starters, oh, and maybe some cake, too, if we feel like it. We're as posh as anyone here now!'

The girls wove through the crowd until they spotted a small tearoom set back from the track. Inside, waitresses in starched white aprons served tea and scones to ladies in furs and silk dresses.

Daisy walked up to the entrance, smoothed down her dress and did her best to neaten her plaits. She gave Edith a confident nod as they walked in arm–in–arm.

A waitress quickly bustled over, 'Are you looking for someone, dear?' the woman asked as she gave them a gentle smile.

'Oh, no thank you,' Daisy answered in her most sophisticated voice. 'My father suggested that my companion and I take tea whilst we wait for Big Red's race.'

'Certainly, dear,' the waitress said as a small smile played on her lips. 'Come this way. It's truly an exciting day, isn't it?'

'Magical,' Daisy said as she and Edith pulled their chairs up to a table for two.

'Now, my name is Rose, and what can I get you little misses?' the waitress asked.

'High tea for two, if you please,' Daisy said.

'Are you sure?' Edith whispered, 'Can you afford that?' She looked at Daisy with concern.

'Look,' Daisy pointed to the menu, 'it's four pence each, and that will leave us some money to buy a treat for Harry as well.'

Rose nodded. 'High tea it is then.'

Daisy swung her feet happily under the table and looked around. Bunches of pink and mauve roses in crystal vases were dotted about. There was a low murmur of conversation and the tinkle of china as ladies sipped their tea.

Edith reached across the crisp linen tablecloth to clutch Daisy's hands. 'This is the most exciting thing ever.'

'Careful, dear.' Rose was back with a tray that

held a china teapot, delicate cups and saucers, milk and sugar, which she set out before them.

I feel like a queen, Daisy thought to herself as Rose poured hot, golden tea into the dainty floral cups. 'Milk and sugar?'

'Yes, please,' Edith and Daisy said together.

'Did you ever see such a pretty teapot and such sweet little cups?' Edith sighed. 'I'm too scared to touch it in case I break it.'

'Come on,' said Daisy, 'you'll be fine. You cock your little finger out like this, see? And blow gently first.' She pursed her lips and blew at the surface of her cup before taking a tiny sip. 'Oh, how delicious,' she said in her fanciest voice, and gave Edith a mischievous wink.

'Where did you ever learn to be so hoity toity?' Edith asked in amazement as she struggled to stick her little finger out to one side. 'My pinkie has a mind of its own – it won't do what yours does,' she laughed.

'I've been watching all the ladies,' Daisy said.

'You can learn a lot just from watching.'

Rose returned with a high cake stand. 'Here we go, my dears.'

'Oh my . . .' Edith breathed.

'Now, you've got mini éclairs at the top, iced cakes next, chicken sandwiches in the middle, and scones with jam and cream on the bottom. And you just let me know if there's anything else you need.' Rose turned to leave, then came back. 'Oh and this is a special treat from me.' She placed a bowl of strawberries and ice cream in the middle of the table. 'You girls look like you'd enjoy it.' She gave them a kind smile and whisked away before Daisy and Edith could thank her.

'Did you ever . . . ?' Daisy stuttered. 'It's so . . .'

'So *wonderful*,' Edith said and shook her head in awe at the feast in front of them.

I must be in a dream, Daisy thought. I must have fallen asleep at my desk at school and be in a dream. 'Come on, Edith, tuck in!'

Daisy selected an éclair from the top of the

stand and took a bite. It burst, smooth and sweet in her mouth, the richness of the custard coating her tongue. Heaven, she thought.

Edith was munching happily on a chicken sandwich and chocolate cake at the same time. Her mouth was ringed with chocolate crumbs and her eyes were glowing with happiness.

The girls ate happily for half an hour, washing their food down with hot, sweet tea.

'Oh dear,' Daisy said at last, as she leaned back in her chair and patted her belly. 'I don't think I can fit in one more mouthful.'

Edith nodded as she finished the last of the ice cream. 'I know what you mean, but there's still that half a scone there, and some cream. It would be a terrible shame to waste it.'

Daisy chuckled. 'Eat it, you goose – it's all yours.' She watched as Edith happily smeared jam and cream on the scone. She looks just like her old self, Daisy thought.

'Right then,' Edith said as she wiped cream

off her face with her sleeve. 'Hadn't we better find Harry, watch this race and get moving?'

'Oh goodness, yes,' Daisy said. 'I'd almost forgotten.' She stood up and pushed in her chair. 'Let's go.'

The girls paid their bill, thanked Rose for her kindness and wandered out into the sunshine and crowds. They walked back to the spot next to the garden and looked for Harry.

'Oi, where on earth did you get to? I've been running around looking for you everywhere. Actually, never mind that,' Harry said, puffing hard as he ran up to them. 'I've got bigger fish to fry. You'll never believe it, girls.' He was too out of breath to speak properly and had to bend and rest his arms on his legs for a few seconds.

'What on earth, Harry?' Daisy said. 'What's all the commotion about?'

Harry stood up, took a deep breath, then turned to the girls with an enormous grin.

'I went over to the stables, like I said, and I

had a look at the horses and a chat with some of the strappers there, and then one of the horses started to get a bit tetchy, so I went up and started talking to him and rubbing his nose and that and he calmed down . . .' He paused and Daisy wondered if he might be about to cry.

He ran a hand over his face and continued. 'And then the strapper comes up and says to me that I'm a natural for sure, and that if I wanted, I could work for him. No pay to start, but I can bunk with the horses and he'll feed me while I learn the game. What d'you think of that, girls?'

'That is the most wonderful news,' Daisy cried, and clapped Harry on the shoulders.

'You're a champion, Harry Waller,' Edith said, and punched him playfully in the belly. 'Good for you.'

'Oh golly,' Harry said as trumpets rang out again across the course. 'The race! Let's go.'

They ran down the hill, joining a surge of people fighting to get close enough to see

Phar Lap. They pushed into a spot near the fence and Daisy felt a flood of elation as hooves thundered toward them. Suddenly the field of horses, glistening and graceful, flew past, their jockeys resplendent in their multi-coloured silks. The horses were so close Daisy could see their flaring nostrils and the slick sweat on their chests. 'Phar Lap, Phar Lap,' she chanted with the crowd, craning to see the finish line.

'And it's Phar Lap breaking away from the pack now,' the commentator called. 'This classy four-year-old is making all the right moves, and he's out of danger now; it's Phar Lap. Phar Lap has won the Melbourne Cup of nineteen hundred and thirty.'

The crowd erupted in cheers. Daisy reached over and hugged Harry and Edith.

'What did I tell you?' Harry said, glowing. 'Didn't I tell you he was a wonder horse?'

'I'm so pleased we stayed to see that,' Daisy said. 'But now I have to get to Flora.'

'Of course,' Harry said. 'And I'd better get over to the stables before that strapper changes his mind about me.'

'Wait,' said Daisy. 'We had some good luck, too.' She handed him four pence. 'Take this. It's your share of the money that we found.'

'Wow, that's brilliant!' Harry blushed.

'Good luck, Harry,' Edith said. 'You're a good egg.'

'Bye Edith, bye Daisy,' Harry said. 'Good luck to the both of you. Who knows? Maybe you'll see my name in the paper one day, riding a Melbourne Cup winner past the post.'

'I hope so,' Daisy said with a smile. What a perfectly delicious day, she thought, feeling drowsy and content. And soon I'll be with Flora.

As Harry disappeared into the crowd, Daisy looked around to work out how to get back onto the street. 'That's where we came in,' she said, and pointed to metal gates behind them. 'We'll just hop another tram, a fifty-seven I think we need, and that will take us almost all the way to Gertrude Street.'

As they headed toward the gates, Daisy saw something in the crowd that made her stop suddenly. It was a familiar face ... or was it? Could it possibly be him?

'What? What is it?' Edith asked.

'I think ... But I'm not sure ...' Daisy stared hard, but the man had disappeared in the crowd.

'Dad?' she yelled, jostling her way desperately toward the spot where she'd seen him. Was that his hat – over there by the railing? 'DAD!' she screamed desperately, not caring that people were looking.

'Daisy!' Edith cried behind her. 'Wait!'

But Daisy couldn't wait. Where had he gone? Was it even him?

She couldn't be sure, but there was no way she'd risk losing him – not after everything that'd happened. 'Stay here,' she panted over her shoulder at Edith. 'Wait for me – I'll be back.'

'You'll never find me!' cried Edith, and followed as Daisy plunged back into the crowd, dodging and sprinting and dodging again. She ducked under the arm of a lady holding a parasol, almost slamming into a man with a top hat who was peering through some binoculars. 'I say – watch it!' he called, but Daisy could barely hear anything above her rasping breath and Edith's footsteps, which were still behind her. 'Dad!' she shouted hoarsely. 'Daddy?'

There! Over there by the bookie's table. Was that him? Come on – faster, she willed her legs, which were trembling with the effort.

'Careful there, girly,' a man cried as she ran straight into him.

'*Daisy?*'

Daisy looked up in shock as Edith banged into the back of her.

'Aren't you the girl I took to the orphanage not two months ago?' It was Bluey, the policeman who had found her at Dudley Flats.

'Run!' Daisy yelled back to Edith. She tried to bolt but Bluey grabbed her by the shoulder. Another policeman took hold of Edith.

'Looks like we've found us some escaped orphans,' the policeman said.

'Let go,' Edith cried, struggling to break free.

'We're not doing anything wrong,' Daisy implored. 'We're just trying to find our families.'

Bluey shook his head. 'Nothing I can do about that, I'm afraid. I have to follow the rules.' He led the way to the carpark, holding firmly to Daisy's arm, and soon she and Edith were bundled in the back of a police car and on their way back to the orphanage.

'But Bluey, please, you've got to take us back to the track! *Please*. I think I saw my dad there and he can explain everything. He'll tell you I don't belong in an orphanage. I told you before – I'm not really an orphan. My sister's living in Gertrude Street with my aunt and uncle, and I was just on my way there, honest.'

'Oh, really, is that so?' Bluey answered, and turned from the driver's seat to look at her. 'So what the devil were you doing at the Melbourne Cup all by yourselves? And what do you mean you *think* you saw your dad? Surely you know your own dad when you see him?'

'It was just for a second and I couldn't be sure, but if you take us back I can find him.'

'And I want to find my brother,' Edith said, her voice tight. 'Please don't make us go back to the orphanage. If I go back I'll never see him again.'

'Sorry, girls,' Bluey said. 'Daisy, we can't go wandering through thousands of people at the Cup in the hope that one of them might be your dad. It's my job to follow the law and that means taking you back right now.'

To have been so close and not to know if she really had seen Dad was too much for Daisy. She rested her head back on the seat and began to cry, quietly at first, but then louder. She wasn't just crying for Dad, and Flora, and

Jimmy, and Amelia, and the life she would never get back. She was crying for Edith, and Freddy, and all the children whose lives were so sad and loveless.

Half an hour later, the car pulled up outside the orphanage. Daisy and Edith stumbled up the stairs.

'She's going to murder us,' Daisy said quietly, wiping her eyes.

'Yep,' Edith sighed.

Miss Dunham met them at the door. 'Well, if it isn't our little runaways,' she said, her voice as cold as steel. 'And where's the other one?' She looked over at the police car. 'There was a boy as well.'

'We just found these two,' Bluey said. 'But I don't think they've done any real harm, Miss. They just wanted to find their families.'

Daisy shot him a grateful look.

'Thank you, Officer, but I will be the judge of that,' Miss Dunham snapped.

Bluey gave Daisy a rueful look and went back to his car. Daisy and Edith followed Miss Dunham back to their dormitory.

'Now,' she said, 'here are your toothbrushes to scrub with. As you can see, the washroom floor is a disgrace. The lavatories also need a thorough clean. You will not go to bed until you're finished, and you can forget about having any dinner. You will be on double chores for the rest of the month and you will not be allowed to leave this dormitory except for meals and chores.'

'What about school?' Daisy asked.

'You will no longer go to school,' Miss Dunham answered. 'From now on, you will both do the work of Day Girls. An education would clearly be wasted on you.'

With that, she stomped out of the room. Daisy and Edith reluctantly picked up their toothbrushes and started cleaning.

10
A Big Shock

AISY's bottom had gone numb on the hard wooden bench. Her eyes were drooping and she had to keep shaking herself awake. She'd only had a few hours sleep after yet another long night scrubbing the washroom floor. My hands are still as wrinkly as prunes, she thought, looking at her aching red fingers. She felt Edith's body start to slump beside her and wiggled in her seat to wake her friend up.

Another stupid Sunday morning waiting for visitors who never come, Daisy thought. I know Mabel and Elsie won't be here, not after the last time when Miss Dunham refused to let them see me. She sighed loudly.

Two weeks had passed since their failed escape attempt. Christmas was just over a month away, and then Flora would be leaving for Sydney. I can't bear to think of her alone in another strange city, Daisy thought. She shifted on the wooden bench again. How I wish Dad would just fling open that door, burst in and tell me he's got Flora and we're going back to the farm. That would be perfect. She knew now that it couldn't have been Dad at the Cup. There was no way he would have been in the city and not come to see us, she thought.

The front door opened and a couple stood in the doorway before a Day Girl showed them into the Superintendent's office, but Daisy was so caught up in her own thoughts that she barely noticed them. The Cottage Mothers will be watching Edith and I more closely now I suppose, she thought, but surely there must be another way to escape?

Edith started to snore, resting her head on Daisy's shoulder. 'Wake up,' Daisy hissed.

'Daisy Sanderson,' a stern voice called.

'Oh, for goodness sake! All I said was two little words.' Daisy looked up expecting to see the angry face of Miss Dunham, but instead Miss McCracken was beckoning to her.

'Ummm,' Daisy said in confusion and pointed to herself. 'Me?'

'Are there any other Daisy Sandersons here?' Miss McCracken said.

'Ah . . . no,' Daisy answered and got up slowly from the bench, trying to stretch some life back into her tired legs.

'Hurry up then, girl, we don't have all day.'

Daisy stumbled up the hall, the stares of the children following her slow walk.

'Come in here, Daisy,' Miss McCracken said, pushing her into the Superintendent's office. 'Come and meet your new parents.'

HOW I BECAME AN AUSTRALIAN GIRL

Michelle Hamer

I was born in a hospital where geckos ran across the walls and monkeys played outside the windows. The hospital was in a country called Malaysia. My parents lived in Malaysia for three years because my dad was in the Australian Army and the army sent him there.

I came to live in Australia when I was two, and my parents and brother and I lived with my grandparents and aunty in a big double-storey house near the sea. Like Daisy, we had lots of pets. A few years later my little sister was born, and I took care of her the way Daisy takes care of Flora. Even though Daisy's life was very different to mine, and very different to yours today, the one thing that never changes for Australian girls is the importance of family.

HOW I BECAME AN AUSTRALIAN GIRL

by *Lucia Masciullo*

I was born and grew up in Italy, a beautiful country to visit, but also a difficult country to live in for new generations.

In 2006, I packed up my suitcase and I left Italy with the man I love. We bet on Australia. I didn't know much about Australia before coming — I was just looking for new opportunities, I guess.

And I liked it right from the beginning! Australian people are resourceful, open-minded and always with a smile on their faces. I think all Australians keep in their blood a bit of the pioneer heritage, regardless of their own birthplace.

Here I began a new life and now I'm doing what I always dreamed of: I illustrate stories. Here is the place where I'd like to live and to grow up my children, in a country that doesn't fear the future.

WHAT LIFE WAS LIKE IN

Daisy's Time

IN the Melbourne Museum, you can see a scrapbook that was put together by a lady called Marie Davie. The scrapbook is full of newspaper clippings and pictures to do with Phar Lap, the famous racehorse. Marie wrote poems to Phar Lap, and her friends knew all about her project and often gave her things about him to paste in. In the 1930s, Marie Davie wouldn't have been alone in her love of the great horse. It was partly because of the era he lived in that Phar Lap became so famous and adored.

As you will know from Daisy's story, the Depression was a terrible time for most people in Australia. It was a time of hardship and despair, unemployment and starvation, uncertainty and struggle. In these dark days, Phar Lap was like a star of hope. His success gave people something to cheer about, talk about, focus on and dream about. They looked forward to his races, and felt proud that the world's greatest racehorse was from Australia (well, he was actually from New Zealand, but he was trained and raced in Australia, so we claim him as our own!). Life didn't seem quite so bad when he broke a record or had a race coming up. Phar Lap brought the whole country together, untied in wonder, affection and excitement.

So when he got sick and died in 1932 while he was racing in the United States, the country grieved as if they had lost someone in their family.

Dudley Flats Mansion

WEST MELBOURNE

A 'Dudley Mansion'. The kitchen is the front room, behind is the
bedroom, which is papered with blue bills (salvaged from the tip, the
print side being turned inward). No blankets, but cleanly washed bags.
The room on the left built for a young man fallen on hard times – so
he is lodged free and meals are also given to him by the owner – till
recently a sustenance man – the generosity of the poor.

DID YOU KNOW THESE THINGS ABOUT PHAR LAP?

Phar Lap won 37 of his 51 races.

The name Phar Lap came from the Zhuang and Thai word for 'sky flash'.

Compared to the average 3.2kg, Phar Lap's heart weighed a whopping 6.2kg!

The horse was a national hero, and lifted Australian spirits during the Depression era.

There is a question about Phar Lap on the Australian Citizenship test.

Criminals tried to shoot Phar Lap in 1930 before his Melbourne Cup win, but missed.

Phar Lap was so good that some bookmakers refused to take bets on his races.

The champion horse died under mysterious circumstances in Mexico at just 5 years of age.

Phar Lap's taxidermied body is now the most popular attraction at the Melbourne Museum. His heart is at the Institute of Anatomy in Canberra and his skeleton is in the Te Papa New Zealand National Museum in Wellington.

Want to find out more?

Turn the page for a sneak peek at Book 3

Daisy staggered backwards in shock and accidentally banged her head against the timber-paneled wall of the Superintendent's office.

What did Miss McCracken mean? How could these strangers be her new parents?

'Oh, goodness! My dear girl, are you all right?' A woman sitting in front of the Superintendent's desk, stood up and stepped toward Daisy, her peach silk dress swishing softly as she moved.

'I'm Mrs Bailey,' she said, and stroked

Daisy's cheek with one gloved hand. 'Are you all right, dear?'

She has such blue eyes, Daisy thought, as the woman gave her a concerned look. Like the cornflowers we had on the farm.

'I'm afraid we've shocked you, dear,' the woman said, and gave Daisy a warm smile.

'It's just, well, I…' Daisy mumbled, too confused to think straight.

'Oh, she's all right,' Miss McCracken said. 'She's got a hard head, that one.'

Daisy rubbed the back of her head and felt the lump that was swelling under her hair. Surely they don't really think they can adopt me. No one can adopt me! I have a father. I have a sister. There must be some mistake.

Follow the story of your favourite
Australian girls and you will see that there
is a special charm on the cover of each book
that tells you something about the story.

Here they all are. You can tick them
off as you read each one.

 ♥
Meet Grace

 ♥
**A Friend
for Grace**

 ♥
**Grace
and Glory**

 ♥
**A Home
for Grace**

 ♥
MEET LETTY

 ♥
LETTY AND THE
STRANGER'S
LACE

 ♥
LETTY
ON THE LAND

 ♥
LETTY'S
CHRISTMAS

 ♥
Meet Poppy

 ♥
*Poppy at
Summerhill*

 ♥
*Poppy and
the Thief*

 ♥
*Poppy
Comes Home*

 ♥
Meet Rose

 ♥
Rose on Wheels

 ♥
*Rose's
Challenge*

 ♥
Rose in Bloom

Peatie's Ghost   Peatie the Spy   Peatie's Pet Rescue   Meet Peatie

Daisy on the Road   Daisy in the Mansion   Daisy All Alone   Meet Daisy

Ruby of Kellie Farm   School Days for Ruby   Ruby and the Country Cousins   Meet Ruby

A Lesson for Lina   Lina at the Games   Lina's Many Lives   Meet Lina

Peacetime for Alice   Alice at Peppermint Grove   Alice and the Apple Blossom Fair   Meet Alice

Nellie's Greatest Wish   Nellie's Luck   Nellie and the Letter   Meet Nellie

Pearlie's Pet Rescue

It's 1941 and school is almost over – not just for summer, but forever. Darwin could be bombed any day, and everyone is leaving for a safer place. Animals and pets of all kinds are being left behind, and Pearlie can't bear it. But can she rescue them all? And what will happen when it's her turn to leave the home she loves?

Follow Pearlie on her adventure in the second of four exciting stories about a courageous girl in a world at war.

Gabrielle Wang is the much-loved author of many popular books for young people, including the Pearlie and Poppy books in the Our Australian Girl series. Her most recent novel for middle readers is the lyrical fantasy *The Wish Bird*.